BURNISHED BRIDGE

Real love is worth the wait

Ray

Ray Mel[illegible]

BURNISHED BRIDGE

A Novella

Ray Melnik

iUniverse, Inc.
New York Bloomington

BURNISHED BRIDGE

This is a work of fiction. All of the characters, names, incidents, organizations, and dialogue in this novel are either the products of the author's imagination or are used fictitiously.

The cover art, book design and author photograph were done by ntech media design

The novella is set in Monroe, Washingtonville, Salisbury Mills, Cornwall, and Tuxedo Park, New York, in the lower Hudson Valley. The specific places and people in this novella are fictitious. All other landmarks and locations described in this novella are real.

iUniverse books may be ordered through booksellers or by contacting:

iUniverse
1663 Liberty Drive
Bloomington, IN 47403
www.iuniverse.com
1-800-Authors (1-800-288-4677)

ISBN: 978-1-4502-1727-9 (sc)
ISBN: 978-1-4502-1728-6 (ebk)

Printed in the United States of America
iUniverse rev. date: 03/04/2010

For that diverse group of individuals with one thing in common: they call me friend.

Acknowledgements

Special thanks to Joann Horai for her creative editing and wonderful suggestions.

Thanks to Edward Hayman for his edits and personal discussions that help me grow as a writer.

Thanks to Ingrid Michaelson whose song, "Maybe", from the album, "Everybody", inspired the idea for the story.

Thanks to Angelina, who sparked my interest in music again when she told me about the Michaelson, album.

Prologue – Burnished Bridge

No matter how successful we are in life, any satisfaction gained from all our achievements is diminished without someone with whom to share them. Life becomes nothing more than an exercise void of color. Love is the greatest gift the cosmos gives us and makes living this life worthwhile. Still, some will never know the feeling, either by choice or by circumstance. Real love starts with attraction that then develops into a deep friendship and respect for one another. In this one life we have to live, nothing can ever be as moving or as strong. I don't believe in fate, so there's really no guarantee that I or anyone else will ever find the one, but I won't stop trying. As Carl Sagan said, "For small creatures such as we the vastness is bearable only through love."

In *Burnished Bridge*, Alex Dael is successful beyond his wildest expectations, but he still feels empty inside. When he reaches the pinnacle of his scientific career, he realizes that it's the search and not the outcome that fuels him. He had been able to hide behind his desire for discovery, but now without it, he clearly sees the hole in himself. Then life plays the cruelest trick of all on him. He meets a woman, who stirs everything inside him, but she's far too young for him and she's with someone else. What's worse is that the man she's with treats her badly. Alex never experienced feelings this deeply before. He's driven by his heart and not his head. His desire to see her turns quickly into hurt. Rather than face the constant reminder of a career that has peaked and the love he cannot have, he decides to walk away from it all.

Alex believes it is because of us, the cosmos comes to know itself. This time it returns the favor.

Burnished Bridge is set in the same towns as my two previous novels, *The Room*, published in 2007, and *To Your Own Self Be True,* published in 2009. The story stands alone, but those who have read my novels will recognize cameo appearances of a few of the previous characters.

The Room
Publisher – iUniverse Inc. 2007
ISBN-10: 0595470297
ISBN-13: 978-0595470297

To Your Own Self Be True
Publisher – iUniverse Inc. 2009
ISBN-10: 1440128588
ISBN-13: 978-1440128585

For additional information, visit: www.emergentnovels.com

Burnished Bridge

I feel numb, I accept that I'm awake, but my vision is distorted and I can't hear. Where am I? What am I doing on the floor? What is that shape moving my way? My name is Alex. I know my name is Alex. It's getting closer. I feel it wrapping around me. The numbness is beginning to fade and I can feel someone's arms. My vision is still unclear, but I hear something.

"Alex."

Monday June 21st 2010

My alarm radio went off to the Ingrid Michaelson song, "Maybe," and I reluctantly crawled out of bed. Normally, on my way to the bathroom, I would shut the alarm off, but instead I just lowered the volume a bit. Five hours of sleep is usually enough for me, but I woke so many times during the night that I wasn't paying attention to what I was doing and cut myself shaving. I stripped off my night pants and underwear, turned on the shower faucet and, while waiting the few moments for the temperature to stabilize, I weighed myself. I stepped into the water and let it run over my head and I glanced down to see the blood from my cheek mixing into the water as it spun and poured down the drain. I could feel the sting, when the water hit the spot, but once I avoided a direct hit to my face, the softened water felt calming. When I finished, I dried off and hung the towel on the bar, but seeing blood spots, I threw it on the floor.

I hadn't experienced even one day of nervousness during the last seven years working on Project Glint, until now as we begin the trials. I can remember the moment I stumbled on the equation that proved the possibility. It was as beautiful as any equation I have ever seen. Barely a month after I published, the Department of Defense visited and declared my work to be a matter of national security. I knew they were right, given the potential. Dr. Greene quickly jumped in and seized the opportunity to secure open ended funding for my research with the goal of putting the theories to practical use and providing a generous salary for me. I made a lot of progress during the first three years, but the key mechanism needed to bring it all to fruition remained elusive, until I took on the assistance of Elina.

Dr. Elina Maina's expertise in magnetic shields was critical. Thirty-two years old, twelve years my junior, I admire how far she had come for what is considered a young age for her field. Elina has an inner spark of excitement in her work. She's tall with long light brown hair and because of her youthful appearance, she often doesn't get the respect she deserves. Boy, are our colleagues in for a surprise.

I envy Elina in that she is able to stay fully engaged in work and still make time for her husband, Truman, and their daughters, Tasha and Nadia. Tasha was one year old when Elina joined the project and Nadia was born two years ago. I was honored when they asked me to be her Godfather. Truman, Elina and I have become really good friends. Elina's contributions to the project are priceless, but I also couldn't have a more pleasant work partner.

I finished dressing and, while making coffee, I opened the cabinet to insert the Michaelson CD, so I could listen again to the song that woke me, kept it low and switched the sound to the speakers outside to listen as I drank my coffee on the deck in back. My house is at the top of a small hill above Beaver Dam Lake in Salisbury Mills; the dam itself is just to the right. The water was almost motionless this morning; barely a breeze touched the trees. The back trees mirrored on the lake and were beginning to drop spring seeds that speckled the reflection. No photograph could ever capture the real essence of such a convergence of calm and beauty. By this stage in my life I hoped to have someone to share it all with me, but Amelia just wasn't the right choice for my wife. I never stopped feeling that something was missing, until I realized it was the love. It wasn't much more than a year after I got the position at SciLab and we moved to Orange County that she decided she wasn't happy with a rural life. Because I grew up on Manhattan's upper west side, I gladly accepted the change; in fact, I desired it. Since my parents passed away, there was nothing really to keep me there. My profession could have taken me anywhere, but at least we were close enough to visit friends in the city and Amelia's family and friends on Staten Island. But it wasn't good enough for her. I kept the condo that my parents left to me; so, during the settlement I gave her what she wanted when I signed it over to her. For Amelia, to live on the upper west side of Manhattan was to live on top of the world. Neither one of us has called the other since then.

There was still time before I had to leave, so I poured a second cup of coffee and went to my desk to pay some accounts online. I automate every payment I can. Maybe it's a part of my geekness, but to me it just makes sense to optimize my time. Bills really irritate me, when they require intervention, but that's starting to change with some companies beginning to offer automatic withdrawal from my account. Once my town began to pull quarterly and yearly taxes, it left only a few utilities to get onboard. A macro I wrote flags any abnormalities and e-mails alerts to me. With the secured dividends that continuously accumulate in my account; I envision the day when I will never need to look at another bill. I took a peek at my retirement funds and SciLab stock, which looked to be doing fairly well, since coming out of the recession. Finally, I checked messages only to unleash a flooding of spam. Oh, look; my ship has come in. I've been offered another fifty million dollars by a Nigerian prince. Now if I could only find a decent spam filter. I hit the delete key repeatedly until my inbox was empty, then it was time to go. There was no need for even a light jacket on such a beautiful June morning, so I slipped out, locking the door behind me.

I stopped at the light to make a left onto Route 208 and saw Brice in front of his tavern scraping the paint flakes off the front door frame. His place always looks well maintained. It has an Old English décor with a large shelf high on the wall behind the bar filled with the countless oddly shaped bottles he loves to collect. It has become my place of choice. So many times I passed that tavern and never thought it would be a good place for lunch. In the past I had lunch in a few places in Monroe, and once or twice a year at Newburgh Marina, but one day a couple of months ago I overheard someone talk about Brooks being a well kept secret, so I went for lunch. I've been going there every day since. I opened the passenger window to say good morning and that I would see him for lunch as usual. He heard me and looked just as the light turned green. He sported the classic Brice smile at a time of day that most people are just trying to wake up.

As I drove along the familiar road to SciLab, I reflected that since my divorce I'm finally getting used to being alone, but the feeling of loneliness comes in waves. I've tried a few attempts at dating, give up and then bury myself in work only to try again. I refuse to give up my contention that there is someone out there for me. No matter how much success I achieve, to live without love is to live in true poverty. But for now, I bury myself in work again. I bury myself in a secret of how beautiful the world really is, with a universe so incalculably immense that no god I've heard of would be capable of creating such awe. All we know so far is that natural continuous evolution is evident in the brush strokes. Our existence is a chance for the cosmos to discover itself, but only if we open ourselves up to look. Most people choose to live behind a veil containing a tiny idea of the universe. They're unwilling or unable to see themselves as they truly are, or the cosmos for what it really is. But I want to see the realities. I want to take that one step further to add my tiny brush strokes through Glint. The math works. Tomorrow we begin putting it to the test.

I entered the gate and drove around to the back of the campus where our lab is located. Originally an astronomy lab, it has a retractable roof and side wall facing Shawangunk Mountain. A better astronomy complex was constructed not far down the back road. Glint went from drawing board to construction last year, and when the new astronomy lab was completed, there were four happy people; Jordan, Hailey, Ella and Adrian. Elina and I were equally happy to get this lab they left behind. Elina and I are closer with them than any of the others at SciLab, since we occupy the only two remote buildings. I never met four co-workers from such diverse backgrounds who could do their work as such a cooperative.

Our target site for Glint was an off campus area on Shawangunk Mountain just across the valley. It consists of a square kilometer of the forest under an outcropping of rock halfway up. It's fenced in for testing and to discourage questions from hikers; the signs posted all around the target warn of an imminent rock slide. The trees easily hide our target pad.

As I turned into the lot, I was surprised to see Elina's car out front, given that I usually arrive first. Since completing the prototype,

I've noticed her growing a little more apprehensive. I swiped my card key and opened the door to find all the lights off in the main hallway. The lab's main lights were off as well and I could see Elina typing away at her station using a small desk lamp over her hand written notes. She knew I was there once she saw the hall lights go on and I stood at the door by the switch for a moment. When she heard me, she still didn't look away from the screen.

"Good morning, Elina. Do you mind if I turn on the lights?"

"Not at all. Go ahead," she said, again not turning her head.

The one main switch controls a series of lights that turn on in sequence rather than all at once, so there was the sound of relays that clicked with each. The space is cavernous with most of the test equipment close to the entrance, opposite the retractable wall and roof. The motors and blowers were installed in the back, so that the distance could minimize the unwanted sound. The electrical storage array blocked some of the sound as well with its five foot high cylinders.

"You're here early," I said.

"Alex, I think I can smooth the ride with a few minor changes that I worked on last night," she replied, still not looking up.

"Not the usual Sunday with your family?"

"Truman took the girls to see their grandparents in DC. He knows how incredibly important these first tests are and he wanted me to have time to concentrate. You don't look the least bit nervous. Aren't you just a little worried?"

“A little. I woke up a lot during the night, but other than that,” his voice trailed off.

“Well, you look perfectly calm,” she said after finally looking up.

“It’s lack of sleep. Would you like a cup of coffee?”

“I had two already, but sure.”

I went to the counter and poured two cups from the pot Elina made earlier and handed her one.

“It’s just an apple you know.”

“But will it be apple sauce at the target?,” she said and smiled.

Glint is designed to take an object, encase it in a magnetic “bottle” and excite the shell with Alfven waves. The shell then causes the atomic matter within to resonate until the bonds that hold its structure loosen. A high powered blast is initiated from an array of lasers embedded in a pod located below. Every atom from the base up breaks the bond with the surrounding atoms and attaches itself to a passing photon. When the stream strikes a solid surface at the target, the atoms reassemble in the order first out, first in, rebinding in that same order, base up.

“So, what did you mean by ‘smooth the ride’?”

“Tightening the field will give the atoms more stability when the bonds begin to loosen. It may not be noticeable to Beatrice, when we finally send her, but with more stability there will be even less of a chance that any of the atoms will move out of sequence.”

“How is Beatrice this morning?”

"I feel bad. I went right to work and didn't check on her yet."

Beatrice is a ten year old Borneo Orangutan, just over a meter tall and intelligent to say the least. Her coat is a rusty red around her very round face. When we let her into the lab, she has a habit of handling the objects on the table after she's seen us use them. We acquired her just four months ago for testing and she's grown as fond of us as we have for her. She lives in a large space built right off the north side of the lab. Attached to the covered space is an outside cage with trees for her to play in. Beatrice has free access to go in and out through a hinged flap, although she prefers to stare at us through the long glass pane in the center of the door. As guilty as we feel to leave her in there alone, if she's not fully occupied, she tends to play with too many things in the lab. It once took me a week to find my notebook, when she decided to carry it around like she often saw us do.

"I'll check on her. You can keep working."

I walked to the back and looked into the long glass pane in the center of the door to see her sitting on the platform that was suspended three meters high on the wall. She was peeling back the skin of an orange. When I tapped on the glass, she swung down the rope to the floor and started for the door. I opened it and Beatrice jumped into my arms and began pushing her stubby nose into my ear.

"Beatrice, don't get me wet. What did I tell you about that?"

She looked at me puzzled and snorted into my ear one more time in what seemed to be an act of defiance. I carried her to the work area, held her in one arm and picked up the coffee in the other.

"Good morning, Beatrice," Elina said, but got no response. I think she knows I was here early, but didn't stop to check on her."

"She loves you," I said and Beatrice finally looked at Elina and reached out to touch her hair.

We've been placing her on the pad each morning for the last few weeks in an effort to make her feel comfortable once we begin testing. The pad is round, two meters across. The surface is a smooth thick glass plate with columns surrounding it that house the magnetic arrays. There are eight of them, three meters in height and equally spaced, but the front two retract for us to enter. There are arms attached to each, halfway up and at the top, where a shotgun oscillator points inside to create an Alfven wave. The top is open. It's like the barrel of a gun, once the pad rises, it tilts toward the target and fires. When switched on, the columns produce small clouds as the frigid temperature of the liquid nitrogen in the tubes meet the warm air. The burst of power needed to operate the lasers for Glint is far too much for any grid to provide, so an array of huge capacitors lines the west wall to feed the massive load. It takes 20 hours of charging to produce the current needed for the 30 seconds final discharge. I walked Beatrice inside and asked her to sit there alone this time and she remained calm after the front columns moved into place. The current for the first two test phases comes from the grid, so if we are successful with the apple we could test with Beatrice right away. After getting to know her, I felt a little uneasy with the risk, but it was critical for us to use a subject with complexity.

"So, do you think she's been acclimated enough?" I asked.

"In terms of being comfortable in the physical setting, it would seem so; but the crucial test will be how she responds once the field is generated. Would you like to take a look at the new adjustments?"

I walked behind Elina and looked over her shoulder. She turned and stared at my shirt and smiled.

"What?" I asked.

"You do realize that shirt has lived out its usefulness?"

"It's comfortable," I said and walked over to the closet to grab a lab coat.

"You really need a woman in your life. What's happening with the dating prospects?"

"You had to ask," I said and smiled. It's just not working out. What can I say?"

"You know, Alex, you just don't get out enough. What did you do this weekend?"

"Well I, I relaxed."

"See. Why don't you get out more often? You're always locking yourself up in your house tinkering with your electronics. So how can you expect to meet someone? A nice woman is not going to just knock on your door, you know, unless, of course, you have a thing for bible thumpers."

"Very funny. You know how uncomfortable it is for me. And it's not like there are a lot of options. We pretty much live in the sticks."

"Alex, you're a really nice guy, good looking, successful and you're a giving person, although sometimes to a fault. Any good woman would be crazy not to see it. You just have to stop closing yourself off like that. Visit that Barnes & Noble on Route 300. You could meet someone nice in the reading lounge in front of the Starbucks inside. You can learn a lot about a woman by the books she chooses to read."

"I know you're telling me these things because you care, but I do want to meet someone. It's just that the process is so torturous," I said, smiling to myself that I had a similar conversation with myself driving here this morning. "You remember that woman, Becky, from Goshen. Two dates and she began smothering me. When I told her it wouldn't work out, it took me two weeks to get her to stop sending me e-mail. One message would be angry and the next would say how much she wanted to be with me. That woman, Seda, from Suffern was a blast as well. She spent the whole time at dinner trying to get me to admit the possibility that spirits exist. Both of them were educated women, capable of interesting conversation, but that didn't last long."

"I'm sorry, Alex, I'm mothering. I just want to see you as happy as Truman and I."

"People say that there's always someone who is right for us. But what if in my case she lives a thousand miles away and we never cross paths. That's the possibility they leave out," I said and smiled. We have a lot going on with Glint right now, so maybe it's better this way for a while."

"That one doesn't fly," Elina said and smiled. "Others, including me, need to work hard on our science. You can do your work in your sleep. In fact, I know you do, since from time to time you come in telling me about a change you thought of during a dream."

She really does care about me, but it's still a little troubling because I know she's right. I do tend to keep to myself evenings and weekends, so a little self sabotage is fairly evident.

"Well, Elina; let's do it."

I used a soft cloth and alcohol to cleanse the pad from whatever traces were left behind each time we were getting Beatrice accustomed to sitting inside. I placed the apple in the center, pressed the screen to move the front columns into place and joined Elina already fixated on the monitors. Multiple displays monitored different feeds, including one echoing video capture. One video camera was positioned at eye line between the pad and the apple so it could record the suspension as the magnetic field is generated.

"Your press."

I touched the screen and we heard the liquid nitrogen beginning to climb the columns. When it reached the top, the field started to strengthen and we both smiled, when the apple rose and remained suspended. The monitor revealed it had risen 17.7799 millimeters above the pad and held there. The oscillators turned on and began to excite the shell as the measurement lasers continuously sampled the apple's size and mass. The outer most portion of the field began to exhibit signs of a plasma-like coating with the waves rippling the field. The effect passed through the apple to the opposite side, and it was maintained for the time required to loosen the atomic bonds. Although diminutive, there was an increase in size, but not in relative mass. We held it for sixty seconds before cycling down to see the apple lower to meet the pad.

I retrieved the apple, sliced it, put a thin slice on a slide for structural analysis under a microscope and assessed whether there were any changes. There was absolutely no damage. I was tense the whole time, so I sat back on the stool behind me. Elina put her cheek flat to the top of my head and squeezed my shoulders.

"You did it, Alex. So far it works perfectly."

The equation tells us that it will work perfectly with Beatrice, too. I walked Beatrice onto the pad and again it didn't faze her at all. She briefly looked around, when the magnetic field started winding up, but never even noticed as she was suspended. The field must feel no different than the pad. When the wave was activated, she held motionless. The outside sensors showed that she was no longer breathing and I held my own breath for the sixty seconds we kept it on. When the field was cut off, Beatrice began to breathe and move slightly, but she seemed disoriented with a look void of emotion. I retracted the front columns and reached in to pick her up.

"Beatrice, are you still our Beatrice? Can you hear me?"

She struggled at first to look at me, but it was obvious she was having trouble seeing. As the minutes passed, the effects slowly diminished and she was soon back to her old self. After it became obvious that she was okay, Elina and I looked at each other and smiled to a stifled laugh. I carried Beatrice to her room and when I put her down, she acted as if she had been through nothing special.

The veterinarians came into Beatrice's space through the outside entrance, since few people are permitted to see Glint. Glancing at Beatrice as I left, I pulled the cover down over the glass pane in the door, so that the veterinarians couldn't see inside the lab from her space. Elina called the veterinarians, as I returned to the table and asked them to give Beatrice a full physical examination and all results were required to be submitted by this evening. In the meantime, our schedule would remain as is.

Elina knew I would be anxious to get out of the lab for a while, so she glanced at her watch and asked, "Time for lunch?"

"Sounds great, but come with me today. We can talk about tomorrow's test. We reached a real milestone today."

She looked hesitant, but saw that I really wanted to talk.

"OK, why not."

When we walked into Brooks Tavern, Brice greeted us and we sat in the first booth. I remembered what made Elina so hesitant about going out for lunch. She seemed awkward, even with Brice. It's something I don't see when she's with Truman. I imagine he grounds her. A man and his two daughters were just getting up from the middle booth and as they passed, the daughter, who appeared to be twelve or thirteen, stopped and looked at Elina. She seemed curious about Elina's lab coat.

"Do you work at that science place in Monroe?" she asked. Are you a scientist?"

"Yes, we work at SciLab, and, yes, we are scientists," Elina told her.

"Well, I'm going to be a scientist."

Her father turned, when he noticed the conversation and said, "Kaela, please, let's get going. You shouldn't…"

"It's OK," Elina said. It's nice to meet a young lady interested in science. Well, Kaela; I hope you do well."

The girls went over to hug Brice and when they got close to the door, it swung open almost banging into the younger one. A man in his twenties marched right in and as the door swung back almost closed, a small hand and arm gently pushed it open again. It was a woman in her late twenties, thin and cute with long stark black hair, wearing tight deep purple leggings under a short black skirt and black top. She held the door open for the man with his daughters to exit. I kind of knew the two were together, although it was a bit disconcerting after seeing his rudeness. He went straight to the booth behind me and was already looking at the menu. The woman glanced at me as she passed and had a look of pain on her face that she thought she was hiding well.

It wasn't long after Elina and I got our food that it started to get loud in the booth next to us. I saw Brice look up. It was only one voice: a low stern voice, getting louder. That poor woman was being subjected to obvious verbal abuse to the point where Brice came around the counter. I was right there, so I beat him to the table. I gave the man a stare and looked at the woman.

"Are you OK? Do you need help?"

"Hey, who are you? Mind your own business," the man shouted.

"Cale, please," the woman pleaded.

Brice came around me and asked the man to leave. He hesitated, contemplating possible outcomes, and chose to take Brice's advice. As he passed me, he turned and mumbled that I shouldn't stick my nose into other people's business. I called him a coward. After the woman saw that he had gone out the door, she thanked me. Through a look of anguish, she was strikingly beautiful to me. I didn't realize for a moment, but I wasn't looking at her, I was staring. I told her it was no trouble.

"My name is Janine. Janine Tal," she said and reached her hand out.

I reached out as well and shook her hand briefly, "Alex Dael. Nice to meet you."

Janine stared at me curiously, before I went back to sit with Elina, who seemed a bit nervous from the events.

"Nice relaxing place, huh," Elina teased.

"Believe me, this is not the usual."

"Uh huh," she interrupted and laughed.

The events of the afternoon faded, though the sweet image of Janine lingered, as we set up for the first "test to target" scheduled for early morning. There was no use staying at the lab. We could examine Beatrice's test results from home. In the morning, Elina is set to go to Shawangunk Mountain and I will control Glint.

Tuesday June 22nd 2010

I slept like a baby, woke early and I arrived at the lab at five AM. Flipping the large silver toggle switch on the frame, the roof and side wall retracted and I calibrated the aim to the target. Any solid surface would cause materialization, but for a better visual record, at the remote site we installed a three meter by three meter white backboard with a white floor surface below.

Because of the angle, the apple will have a meter and a half drop so we placed a cushion below.

I put the apple inside Glint, closed the columns and waited only moments before the video came online. Elina appeared on the monitor and looked a little disheveled.

"Good morning, Elina. Are we taking turns? It looks like you couldn't sleep this time."

Seeing herself in the monitor, she patted down some unruly hair sticking up from her head and told me, "I got about an hour and a half all together. I didn't get to look at the test results for Beatrice until late. I'll be fine. I bought three coffees this morning. So you saw, she got a clean bill of health."

"Yes, it all looked good. If you're set, we are ready to go here," I said and she nodded affirmatively.

Neither of us said anything as we initiated the steps one by one. This time, when the magnetic field was generated, the pad lifted and turned toward the target. The apple remained fixed as the oscillators turned on. About ten seconds later, the lasers fired and I couldn't take a breath. The three seconds indicator sounded and I kept my eyes on the apple, holding back any blink.

The blast was blinding, but I could still see the apple's structure disperse into the light. On the target monitor, I saw the structure restored almost instantly as the light struck our back board and the apple dropped to the cushion. Elina put her face to the camera and screamed at me.

"Did you see that? It's here, Alex. Did you see the granulation? It's here and it's not apple sauce!" she yelled and smiled.

My voice became excited, "I'm setting the system for recharge. I hate that it takes twenty damn hours before we can test with Beatrice. Let's get a look at the apple when you get back."

We later found the apples structure entirely intact.

It was half past eleven, when I decided to go for lunch. I asked Elina to come with me again, but she said that she wanted to lie down in the lounge for a while, having had little sleep. There wasn't much we could do between tests, so we agreed that I would wake her at three to ready for Beatrice's test in the morning.

Brice was alone, when I walked in. His bread and butter came from his afternoon regulars, but a few people will be coming for lunch soon. What I like most is that it's still a well kept secret. I walked down to the far end of the bar where Brice had a stool he sat on between serving.

"Hi, Brice; May I have a crab salad sandwich and orange juice, please, on whole wheat."

I could see straight into his kitchen from where I was and he left the door open as he prepared my lunch.

"You look really happy today, Alex. It's nice to see that. Did you meet someone?"

"No, it's not that," I said smiling. Seven years of work and the first full test was successful this morning. I wish I could tell you more, but you know, its top secret stuff. So, how was that woman, Janine, after we left yesterday? I felt bad for her."

"She was OK. She told me that he just started being that way and says she is sure he's just going through a bad time. Personally, I don't think guys like him ever change. She rented the second floor, two buildings down. She tutors high school kids from four to six and college students at different times during the day. We occasionally talked on the street, but yesterday was the first time she came in for lunch."

I was eating my sandwich and Brice was in back, when I felt a gentle hand on my back. I turned and saw Janine. Her apologetic look soon changed to a smile and she sat on the stool next to me.

"I'm sorry about Cale yesterday. He's not normally like that. Your sandwich looks good. Maybe I'll try one of those. Orange juice, huh? Nothing in there right?"

"You mean alcohol? No, I don't drink very often; maybe at a wedding or a glass of wine from time to time with dinner. Getting a little personal, aren't we," I said and she laughed.

Brice soon came out greeting Janine and made the sandwich for her just before others started coming in for lunch.

I have to ask, "Your hair is blacker than I've seen. Can I ask what your family heritage is?"

"My mother is Palestinian and my father is an Israeli Jew. My dad had an offer to teach at NYU and he accepted. I was born two years later. Once my dad retired they moved to New Windsor and I moved up to be near them. They're all I have and I'm all they have. Both sides of the family disowned them. It tears at both of them to see all the hatred still festering there."

She and I got lost in the conversation. She spoke what could have been my thoughts, but I just listened. Time passed until one moment she looked up at the clock.

"I have a student coming at one-thirty and I lost track of the time. I have to go. I really enjoyed talking with you, Alex. I'm sure we'll talk again."

Janine left and the place began to empty again, so Brice came to sit on his stool. He noticed that I stayed longer today and I explained about how Elina needed to nap, given that she hadn't slept all that well.

Brice gave me a funny look and said, "Nothing to do with Janine, right?"

He made me nervous and I felt a little defensive, when I said, "Brice, I'm forty-four. Janine is what, at most in her late twenties? And in a relationship on top of that."

He just smiled at me. He hit a nerve, though.

When I returned to the lab, I sat at my desk and began examining the data. I woke Elina at three and she seemed to benefit from the few hours of napping. We finished all the calibrations for morning and took Beatrice out for a while. Elina asked now that we are so attached to her, did I feel guilty subjecting her to such a risk. Of course, I did, but I felt confident enough now that I would test it on myself, if allowed. With Truman and the girls still away, Elina was in no rush to leave, but I told her to go relax and try to get a good night's sleep. Tomorrow it was her turn in the lab and mine at the target site.

Wednesday June 23rd 2010

I saw the clock on the dashboard change to five-twenty AM, as I was traveling up the gravel road toward the target site. The sky looked so clear, not a puff of a cloud as far as I could see. I opened the padlock to the fence and closed it behind me. It's a short walk from the gate to the equipment mounted just beyond the trees. It took a few minutes to pull back the tarp and power on the remote camera system. The view of the lab side of the feed showed Elina at the station running through system checks. When I checked the line of sight, I saw the lab in the distance with a glimmer of sunlight reflecting off a few of the steel caps on the columns.

"Good morning."

"Hi, Alex. Beatrice is already making herself at home in the lab. She was happy to see me this morning."

I could see Beatrice pass the camera and sit on my usual stool next to Elina. She was staring at the monitor and touching the glass as I spoke. When it was time to test, I asked Beatrice over the link if she would sit on the pad and she walked over to Glint and sat in the center. Elina went over there and took a moment to speak gently to her, just so she would hear a calming voice. Phase one began and when Beatrice was suspended and frozen, the body of Glint lifted up and tilted toward the target. We saw the ten seconds mark and then heard the three seconds warning.

The lasers fired and I could see on the monitor the atoms stripping away and almost instantly re-converge at my end. When complete,

Beatrice dropped to the pad and had that same blank look she had after her first test. I sat next to her and held her as she began to come out of it. I squeezed her and kissed her rough forehead.

"That's my girl. You'll never know what kind of history you've just made."

I saw Elina on the monitor just looking at the two of us and smiling. I carried Beatrice to my car and seat-belted her into my back seat for the drive to the lab. She was staring out the window at all the trees. To her, it must have looked like an immense playground. As I opened the front door to the lab, she ran ahead through the hall and plopped herself down in my seat again. When I turned the corner, I saw her reaching out to Elina for her hug.

"Oh, no you don't, Beatrice. I want my seat back," I said.

I gave Beatrice a bag of fruit and carried her into her room. She still looked calm, as if nothing happened. Elina initiated the re-charge, even though we planned on analyzing all the data for a few days. Having gone through transport, we also wanted a more comprehensive examination of Beatrice before we tested again. Just a few more tests and we could schedule a demonstration with DOD.

At eleven-forty-five AM I invited Elina to lunch again, but she told me to just go ahead. As I pulled into a space in front of the tavern, I saw Janine sitting on the stoop two doors down. She saw me and waved. I stood for a moment at the front of the car, but rather than go right into Brooks, I went over to sit next to her on the step.

"So how are you doing? Did you work things out yet with your boyfriend?"

"Cale just hasn't been himself lately."

"Are you sure it's that?" I said kind of smirking.

"Meaning what?"

"I can't be kind about this. Maybe that's his real self. There's no excuse for acting that way, especially with someone you care about."

"He's just having a bad time at his job. He works for an insurance company in Monroe and they're having it tough with the economy. He told me he wouldn't do it again, and I think he means it this time. I realized that yesterday I talked your ear off about me. So what about you and your girlfriend? She's really pretty."

"Elina? She's not my girlfriend. She's my assistant at SciLab. I've been alone for awhile; a bit busy at the lab."

"Oh. So what do you do?"

"I'm a physicist. The project is classified, but I've been at it for the last seven years," I said and straightened up smiling. "I wish I could give you details, but it's amazing, Janine, and we had our second full test this morning. It works and it works well."

We spoke for over an hour and again, I lost track of time. There is so much depth in her and as we talked I couldn't help staring at her eyes. They were almost as black as her hair and so beautiful. It was so distracting at times that I had to ask her what she just said. Then, we saw a young woman crossing the street and walking our way.

“My one-thirty appointment is early. Hey, you never had lunch. I had a sandwich before you arrived.”

“No worries. I’ll have Brice make me something to take back. Stay happy, OK?”

When I finally got back to the lab, Elina’s lunch was only half eaten next to her on the desk. She looked up at me with a bit of a devilish grin.

“It’s not like you to be gone so long. Plus you do realize you have a very strange happy look on your face,” Elina said smiling.

“I was talking with Janine and just lost track of time. Sorry.”

“It’s fine. A woman, huh? Nice.”

“She’s just the woman who was having trouble at Brooks Monday. I was just being friendly.”

“Uh huh,” she said sarcastically.

“No not you too. She’s too young for me and she’s in a relationship.”

“Well, she would do a lot better with you than that guy at Brice’s.”

“I just can’t and she wouldn’t want me, but I admit that I’ve not been able to get her out of my mind.”

“Well, ask her out, Alex. You don’t know if she cares that you’re older.”

“I don’t know.”

I was happy that we were interrupted by a video IM request from the astronomy lab down the road. I switched it to the large screen and connected. It was Hailey.

“Alex, Elina. You have got to see this. NASA is providing the feed through Hubble.”

She switched the view to a remote feed and we saw a round rim stretching almost half the distance from Jupiter to Ganymede. Almost dead center was what looked to be a planet. Hailey zoomed in and we could clearly see that it was.

“Is that what I think it is,” I asked?

“Yes. The rim is the outer surface of a wormhole and that’s a planet inside that is not in our solar system, of course. Astronomers all over the world are frantically collecting data before the wormhole dissipates. It appeared at around two-fifteen this morning. Even Hubble can’t see clearly through, but initial readings show the signature of all the elements necessary for water, an atmosphere, and even the stuff of life. Everyone is also trying to understand why the wormhole is stable, and how long it might remain that way.”

“That’s amazing,” Elina said and was fixated on the screen image. “Can you keep that feed patched into our lab?”

“Sure. I’ll just leave it up.”

For the next couple of days Elina and I worked on analyzing our data, but were frequently sidetracked by wanting to know more about the planet they discovered. Each new test result returned about the planet was more startling than the last. They were now certain there was water on the planet, and convinced that it has a breathable atmosphere. The mixture of gases suggested that the levels of oxygen must have come from some form of plant life. SETI trained its equipment at the planet, but there were no signals detected to suggest the presence of technologically advanced intelligent life. If an intelligent civilization existed there, it may not be advanced enough to use radio or other more advanced means of communication. Then again, we had no way of knowing whether the waves could even traverse the tunnel, especially given that vision was obscured.

This was such an incredible event, yet even with the information spreading around the globe, our fellow citizens in the US viewed it as nothing more than a novelty. I guess I should have expected that. The popular primetime television shows were more exciting to them, but not Janine. Yesterday and again today over lunch at Brooks, she wanted to know everything I was getting from the feed. Every day since we began talking I realized more and more that I loved everything about her. She's everything I ever wanted in a woman and yet I couldn't have her. At first I was satisfied just talking, but it was beginning to hurt now to the point where I'm even thinking of finding another place to go for lunch. Maybe it would help me get her out of my mind. Last night I even dreamed we were together and it was the cruelest joke life ever played on me.

Elina and I agreed that we would make up some of the lost time analyzing the data over the weekend, so we split up the information and would report on our halves come Monday morning. Our hope was to perform the next test on Tuesday, if we are able to complete the work without being fixated on the wormhole. As fantastic as Glint is, our curiosity was still piqued over such an amazing event. We both planned to VPN into the lab and keep the feed up in our homes. Elina had a third thing to contend with: Truman was retuning home with the girls.

Driving home, I passed Brooks, battling with my feelings and struggling inside not to stop to see Janine when her evening class ended. I didn't stop and for the first time ever my house felt empty and incredibly so. I buried myself in work, but paused every time a new data stream came in from Hubble. By Monday morning they had concluded that the planet was habitable and driving to the lab struck me. We have Glint, and the opportunity to send something there. We would need to find a way to target a land mass. Hitting an ocean would do little good. I couldn't wait to tell Elina my thought.

Monday June 28th 2010

I arrived at the lab before Elina and spent the time before she came reviewing the data collected about the planet. I was just starting to look if land masses or oceans could be plotted, when Elina walked in with a huge smile on her face, threw her bag on her desk and came right over to sit on her stool next to me.

"Alex, did you see everything they discovered about the wormhole this weekend? Never mind, of course you did. I can tell by that grin. They're calling the planet, WEP, Wormhole Enhanced Planet. And did you see that they determined the distance? It's symmetrical to us. Yesterday morning they fired lasers in succession then observed which ones hit WEP and whether the composition of the targets hit were liquid or solid. They're crunching the data to get a better number, but it's approximately one hundred and forty light minutes away."

"Had a lot of coffee already, huh," I said laughing, noticing Elina was a little more energetic than usual. "I had a thought I'm really excited about. First, let me ask if you finished your half of the analysis?"

"Yes. Everything looks solid. And yours?"

"Perfect. Elina, I think we should use Glint to send something to WEP." Elina looked astonished. I continued, "We may not be able to tell anyone yet, but we can record it all and share it later. Once they're finished analyzing, we can use the results to locate a land mass so we don't target a mountaintop or an ocean. Just think, we can send an object to another world."

Elina's astonishment changed to a smile and she nodded yes, then said, "Yes. Yes, we should try. You're right. What a unique opportunity. I read the notes from the team and there's every indication the wormhole will remain stable for at least three more days. They estimate it will dissipate once Ganymede goes further out on its elliptical orbit, based on its angle at the wormhole's first appearance."

"What I would really like to do is send Beatrice. To successfully land a primate would give us invaluable information. It would tell us if a living, breathing source could span the distance. It would be the most we could learn, but that is worth the risk."

"But we can't," Elina said a little worried.

"No. Not if we can't be sure. The data shows all the bio-chemical markers for life and a breathable atmosphere, but there's no way to know if the resources where she's sent are sufficient enough for her to survive. We'll prepare a package to send containing a greeting, some science and other objects. There may not be intelligent life to see it, but we would have our bases covered and we will still get some fantastic data from the process itself."

We worked all morning on a message in a bottle, much like a compliment to the Golden Record launched inside Voyager in 1977. To think, it will be another 40,000 years before Voyager is even remotely close to star AC+79 3888 and Glint could shoot across the universe to WEP in just 140 minutes or so. The results came in and we used the mainframe to determine the exact moment to shoot, so our payload would precisely hit a landmass. We will need to aim where the planet will be approximately one hundred forty minutes after we fire, some time around a quarter past three tomorrow morning.

Come eleven-forty-five I thought about getting lunch and grappled with whether I should find another place to eat or go to Brooks. I don't know why I tried to convince myself that I don't want to see Janine, when the final decision maker in my mind does what it wants anyway.

Janine went to Brooks a little early and had Brice all to herself. He's always there to listen, but having a daughter himself made him especially fatherly to Janine. She sat at the stool across from him and placed her bag on the bar. She began rifling through it searching for something and it was taking a while.

"Lost something, have you?" Brice asked.

"I promised Cale I would walk over to the Washingtonville police station to pay for a speeding ticket he got racing away the day you asked him to leave," Janine said, finally pulling some papers from her bag. "I have another break at two o'clock and I'll walk over then."

"So what would you like today?" Brice asked.

"I'm going to wait for Alex, but I'll have what he likes again: that crab salad sandwich and an orange juice."

"You really like Alex, don't you?"

"Well, yeah; sure. He's a great guy," Janine said noticing an unusual smile on Brice's face.

"Oh, you mean, uh, no. I couldn't do that to Cale and even if I wasn't in a relationship, I'm sure Alex feels I'm too immature for him."

"So you do care for Alex. Listen, Janine; I lost my wife when my daughter, Lacie, was still very young, but the time my wife and I had together was priceless and she's still in my heart. Any one of us could be gone in an instant. Is it better to have forty or fifty years with someone like Cale, or thirty with someone who adores you and makes you happy?"

I walked into Brooks and saw Janine at the end of the bar talking with Brice. They both looked toward me and Janine smiled. She was awash in black, with her black hair, dark eyes, tight black shirt and pants. Only her bare face, arms and hands showed. I sat next to her and could smell a beautiful perfume, apparently applied not much earlier.

"The usual, Alex?" Brice asked.

"Yes, thanks, Brice," I said and he walked into the back. "Janine, do you mind taking a booth today? I'm in the mood for a little more room than here. You already told Brice what you're having, right?"

"I told him that I'd like the crab salad again."

We talked until Brice brought over the food, but were mostly silent, once we began eating. From my peripheral vision I caught her staring at me, when she thought I wasn't looking. She seemed a bit anxious today, no, maybe even sad. It was obvious she wanted to hide what was bothering her, which only made me want to be the one to help her. By the time I had to leave, she looked happy again, but was disappointed when I told her I had to get back. Even though I asked her if she'd be here tomorrow, I was sure she would be.

Driving to the lab, a text message from Elina came up on my console. It read, *"Alex, you need to see something. We'll talk when you get back."* I was close enough that I wasn't tortured too long with curiosity. As I walked in, she was replaying a portion of the Hubble feed.

"What did you find?"

"I was looking at the feed from this morning at about ten-twenty-one and watch this."

She froze on a frame and I could see a faint white/red spot on the surface of WEP.

"What the heck is that? Is that what I think it is?"

"It's a laser shot. There's intelligent life on WEP, Alex."

"Unbelievable. Are you sure?"

"Yes. I spoke with Jordan. It's confirmed. The astronomy lab plotted the location to within a meter and a half."

"Elina, we've got to send Beatrice tomorrow morning. We can send the message on Wednesday, if the wormhole remains open. I would much rather have the data from sending her than the message and it's too early in testing to chance sending another object that large in the same stream. Whoever's there is intelligent enough for laser technology, so I'm confident she'd receive care."

Elina looked a little sad, but said, "I know you're right, Alex, but I'll miss her."

"Me, too, but sending Beatrice would provide the data to see if a human subject could one day traverse an expanse without destabilizing. I envision the day when we can equip a space station with a sealed transparent room to which we can send humans. The light would pass through, materializing them safely inside. Elina, it would revolutionize the moon mission. Now that we know there is someone out there, we have to send her."

For the rest of the afternoon we let Beatrice stay in the lab. It was quite a jump from kilometers to light minutes and although the tests are why she's here, I was none the less apprehensive.

"How about we dress her in a space suit and make them think she's the intelligent life here. ...only kidding," Elina said quite out of character.

"OK, who are you? What have you done with my assistant?" I said and laughed.

We used the mainframe to extrapolate the exact time to fire Glint so that Beatrice would hit the plotted target. To assure the preciseness needed, the computer system would have to control of the shot. Elina entered the macro and we decided we'd get some sleep so that we could start at two AM. But leaving early made little difference. I hardly slept and by midnight I gave up and went to shower.

Tuesday June 29th 2010

I had several cups of coffee by the time I left and the caffeine fueled anticipation and gave me my second wind. Entering the lot, I saw that Elina's car was already there. I walked in to find her in the dark again with just the small desk lamp lit as she stared at the screen. I turned the lights on.

"You couldn't sleep either, huh," I said.

"I got about two hours, but no, how could I? Truman is taking care of the girls in the morning. He's such a great guy, Alex. I don't know what I would do without him," she said, but noticed a sad look on my face. "I'm sorry, Alex."

"No. That's great, Elina. Please don't let me stop you from talking about your family. I love hearing about them. It's just been a little tough lately."

"Well, you've been having lunch with Janine every day. Why don't you just ask her out?"

"To tell you the truth, she's the one making it rough. I have to be honest with you, Elina. I can't stop thinking about her and I can't stop wanting to see her. I've never felt this way about anyone before, ever."

"Well, then, why don't you tell her how you feel? Maybe she feels the same way. Why not?"

"She doesn't look at me that way. She wants it to work with her boyfriend, and it kills me because she deserves better. She deserves someone who adores her like I do."

"Now I understand what's been bothering you so much."

"I'll be fine, thanks. I think it's amplified by the fact that I've reached the pinnacle of my career. I've decided I'm going to hand the work over to the DOD once we give our demonstration. You can lead the development, but I'm done. I've got all the money I need and eventually this will go commercial so money will pour in. You, Truman and the girls will never have to worry again either."

Saturday June, 25th 2022

Elina took her cup of tea from the wall panel but set it down on the counter so that she could tie Nadia's hair back in a ponytail. Before the second clip went in, Nadia turned around and her hair slipped from Elina's hand.

"Mom, I don't want to go to French Woods this summer."

"But you love that camp; why not?"

"I want to finish fixing up my new room and Jenny and I have things we plan to do. Besides, Tasha's going away to college in the fall and I want to spend time with her, too."

"Well, it's up to you, sweetheart. Listen; don't forget to charge the portable. I need to be able to reach you. Why don't you just set it on the pad before you go to bed every night?"

"Max and I keep the channel open sometimes as we are going to sleep."

"I really wish you wouldn't do that. You're too young to be limiting yourself to one boy."

"Oh, Mom, things are different in the twenties." Nadia responded in a complaining voice.

Elina looked to the video panel and initiated the Universal Personal Assistant. It was the first release of an advanced system developed at SciLab and was installed just two weeks earlier.

"Beatrice; please read my tasks list for Monday. Display the weather forecast below."

A three dimensional image of a woman with red hair and bright blue eyes appeared on the wall screen. It was difficult to distinguish her from an open channel until she spoke. The voice was a bit rigid, although it seemed to be improving as the days passed.

"Good morning, Elina. Good morning, Nadia."

Beatrice ran through the list and displayed the weather projections at the bottom. She was speaking the last task when Tasha came in with a "Mom you know you love me" look.

"Good morning, Tasha," Beatrice said, looking in her direction.

"Mom, that thing is really starting to creep me out. Can I take your car out for a while? I need to buy a new portable."

"As long as you drop your sister off at Jenny's house first, then fine. Those two have really become inseparable friends. Oh, and take the Volt."

"Mom, please, not that old thing."

"Tasha, its 4th gen... It's only six years old."

"Oh. OK. And don't forget to talk to Benny's boss at the gatehouse. I think he's been coming on to me and that's creeping me out, too. Why do we have to live in Tuxedo Park anyway? What was wrong with our old house?"

"I'll talk with Sergey about Ben. Your dad and I thought you girls would like it here. Give it a chance. I think you'll adjust by the time you leave for college in the fall."

"I like it here, Mom," Nadia said.

"That's because you're only a freshman," Tasha responded. "I had to be ripped away from my friends in the middle of my senior year."

Tuesday June 29th 2010 - continued

Elina was obviously disappointed with my decision to step away from Glint, but I was leaving her with a great career path and my love has always been for the theoretical side. I have no intention of ending up like a television series that goes on for one season too many.

"Alex, I can understand how you feel, but why don't you just take a little time off to think about it more? I know you. You'll just lock yourself away in your house."

"I'll still consult from time to time and you know all the science behind Glint. There's a Dr Kyle Trace, who works in the main building. You might consider asking him to join you. He's a few years younger than you. I don't know what he's working on right now, but his background might make him a good fit."

We finished setting up the system and opened the roof and wall to ready for the shot. I took Beatrice from her room and all she wanted to do was hold me. I explained what we were going to do, knowing full well she had no idea what I was talking about, but she loved the attention. When the time came, Elina and I both gave her a long hug and then I placed her on the pad. The sequence was exact, computing the lead time to target once it came into view. All of the monitoring equipment began to turn on with only minutes left. Beatrice was calm as we talked with her through the columns and then we heard the macro start as the cloud wafted up from the tubes. The wave began and Beatrice was now frozen. The pad lifted then pointed west and up. The three seconds warning sounded and in moments Glint fired its massive burst of light into the sky.

Now all we could do was wait to see an indication that Beatrice hit the target. It will take close to one hundred and forty light minutes to strike and then close to one hundred and forty more before we see that it hit so that we can analyze the stream. If Beatrice materialized, there would be an indication of the light being brighter at the edges around a solid mass. That was all we would get, but that would at least tell us that the stream remained stable and that we had been successful. We were tapped into the Hubble feed and both of us were exhausted from lack of sleep, so we sat back in our desk chairs. With over four and a half hours to wait, I set an alert for ten minutes after seven. I soon did fall asleep and when I woke, Elina was sitting up in her chair staring at the large video feed.

“Did you get any sleep,” I asked.

“Only about an hour. How could I sleep with Beatrice’s atoms flying through the cosmos,” Elina said and smiled.

When the critical time arrived, we watched and saw a tiny reflection of light from Glint as it struck WEP. It hit dead on target. We filtered the light by frequency and intensity, but could never see the variations with our eyes. We needed the mainframe to analyze and verify that there was mass in the center. There was.

"Thank you," I told her. "If the astronomers have it right, tomorrow we'll be able to send our message in a bottle."

With nothing left to do because the package was already prepared, so I told Elina to go home and get some rest. We would meet back here at the same time tomorrow. After that I would set up the demonstration for DOD. She left and I stayed behind to look through seven years of memories in my desk. I was never one to clean out items and in the large drawer to my left I pulled out small objects and little pieces of paper that mean nothing to anyone but me. Buried at the bottom was my worn paperback copy of "The Age of Innocence." I don't know why I never removed it from the drawer, but maybe the loveless marriage had something to do with it. My deciding to leave the development of Glint to others lifted a huge weight, but it was a weight not unwanted. Anxiety and pressure are inherent in a deep desire to succeed, but it keeps me from a meaningless life. To me, it's the challenge of the achievement rather than the success. The absence of one exposes the emptiness of my life beyond these walls. Just after nine AM, I decided to go home.

Saturday June 25th 2022 - continued

Once the girls left, Elina sipped her tea and commanded the monitor to display the public news channel. She heard a call tone and connected video to the astronomy building at SciLab. It was Adrian.

"Elina, remember the wormhole that appeared near Jupiter in 2010? Well, it's back, and so is WEP"

Elina visually stunned, "I'm coming over."

Elina asked Truman to keep an eye on the girls later in the afternoon because she had to go to SciLab. She quickly stuffed her portable in her bag and drove to the astronomy lab. With a direct feed to Space Telescope Sagan, Hailey, Ella and Adrian were at their stations throwing every type of sensor they had at WEP.

"So, when did it reappear?" Elina asked.

"About two-fifteen this morning," Adrian said. "Jordan was working in Norway at the Haagaar Observatory and he woke us up with the news. He's already booked his flight back. Uh, do you ever talk with Alex? I'm sure he would love to see this."

"I don't. I haven't spoken with him since he left the project."

"It seems strange that he would walk away like that."

"Alex was an unusual guy."

Hailey walked over, "No more crude measurements. They already determined it carries the same element signatures as it did in 2010. It's the same planet, but with a slightly higher CO2 content in the atmosphere this time."

Tuesday June 29th 2010 – continued

I napped on my couch, sleeping several hours filled with dreams. During my last one, I was holding Beatrice. I felt her rough rust colored fur and saw the look she gave when she missed me. She pushed herself down to the floor and held my hand outstretched and then let go.

I woke with a renewed sense of purpose, realizing why I dreamed of her. There may never again be the opportunity to put a man on another living world, so I decided to follow Beatrice to WEP. I would need to convince Elina to help me, or at least not try to stop me. If she did assist me, she couldn't breathe a word about it, or it would jeopardize her career.

I was excited about a new lease on discovery. They'll wonder where I went, most especially DOD, so if I was going to save Elina from scrutiny, I had to point them in another direction. The few clues that I would leave would indicate that I hadn't met up with foul play. I went online to cancel my newspaper and oil deliveries, and my electric service, ending a week from today. It would provide proof that it was a conscious decision. There would be little I could do about the house, but the taxes were automatically withdrawn so that the town wouldn't be short changed. They would understand why I didn't take my car, since I didn't want to be found, but in case someone checked, not taking my clothes wouldn't make sense and I would need to withdraw some cash. I stuffed a large black garbage bag with half my wardrobe and threw them in the back of my car. I drove to five corners and went into my bank to withdraw five thousand dollars. I dropped the clothes into a large Goodwill bin out in front of the Price Chopper store and then walked into the Goodwill store nearby and handed two women behind a counter the five thousand dollars. I asked only that they not talk about the donation.

It was almost three o'clock and this was the first day in a long time that I missed going to Brooks for lunch. In fact I missed lunch altogether. But I didn't want to leave without seeing Brice and, hopefully, Janine one last time to say goodbye. I passed my street and drove to Washingtonville. When I arrived, Brice had already cleaned up from the luncheon patrons and was sitting on his usual stool reading the newspaper. He smiled when he saw me.

"I didn't think I'd see you today."

"Elina and I worked during the night so I went home to get a little sleep."

"Are you hungry? Can I make you something?"

"That would be great, Brice. I'll take the usual crab salad sandwich if you have any left."

Brice did, and he handed me a glass of orange juice and left the kitchen door open so that we could talk while he made my sandwich.

"You know, I never saw Janine look so lost without her lunch companion. She's a great girl. Alex, you should..."

"We've talked about this. I can't, Brice. Besides, I have something to tell you," I said and was silent until he walked over with my plate. "I'm leaving town in the morning and I really came to say goodbye."

"Leaving," Brice said kind of shocked. "That's sudden. Elina must be disappointed. What's wrong, Alex? Where are you going?"

"Nothing is wrong. In fact, I haven't been this excited, since I came up with the idea for the work I just completed. I've not told Elina yet, and where I'm going I can't tell you."

"More secrets... I understand. Well, I'll miss having you come by, and I know someone else who will miss you as well."

We heard the front door open, but the light was bright from outside and we couldn't make out who it was until Janine stepped inside.

"Hi, Brice. Hi Alex. I saw your car outside and I don't have a student for a couple of hours. I see you're late for lunch," she said and I smiled.

I asked her to join me in a booth and I carried my food over to sit down. Brice handed Janine an orange juice and told me he wanted to hear more of what we talked about, later. Janine noticed the seriousness in Brice.

"That was a really solemn look. What did you two talk about? Oh, wait. I'm sorry, Alex. It could be personal."

"It's OK. I can't stay long, but I want to tell you. I'm leaving in the morning and I didn't want to go without saying goodbye."

Janine couldn't hide the disappointment. Little did she know that she was one reason why I decided to leave.

"Why are you going? Where are you going?"

"I wish I could tell you, but I can't. Let's just say, I won't be sure of where I'm going myself until I get there. Elina doesn't know yet."

Janine was speechless and just looked down into her glass. Her eyes glazed and it seemed for a moment that she was going to miss me more than as just a friend. But that passed and she looked up.

"I know it hasn't been that long since we met, but I enjoyed talking with you, Alex. I will miss you," she said, this time unable to hold her voice from cracking just a little.

"I will miss talking with you as well, more than you know. Janine, don't settle for Cale. He's not right for you and since I'm going, I can't help but be honest. Personally, I think he's a coward. The way he treated you the day we met will come back. It was Camus who said, 'Nobody realizes that some people expend tremendous energy merely to be normal.' Cale will do it again."

"Thank you for the honesty, Alex. I hear you."

I asked her to excuse me for a moment and I went up to say goodbye to Brice. I shook his hand and he hugged me like a son. I let him know what a good friend he has been. He told me to please come around again in the future, but I knew how impossible that would be. Janine, seeing me say goodbye to Brice, understood I was leaving. She got up to walk me out. We stopped by my car and she startled me when she wrapped her arms around me and squeezed tightly. She ran her hands down my arms to my fingers and held the tips for a moment. This time a tear rolled off her cheek and dropped onto the back of my hand. We didn't say another word and I got into my car and left.

It would be more difficult this night over any other to get sleep, but before I tried, I decided to write a note to absolve Elina of any knowledge and steer them away even more. I thanked Dr. Greene for his kindness and Elina for all her hard work, but said that I had to get away. I told the DOD they had my silence, and that Elina would lead the project moving forward. With sufficient information to throw them off track, I decided it wouldn't be right to spring this on Elina in the morning, plus I could use her help staging it. I rang her home and Truman answered. I could hear Elina talking to the girls in the background, but she soon came to the phone.

"Hi, Alex. I promise I'm going to sleep shortly. When I got back this morning I slept until noon. So, what's up?"

"Are you sitting down?"

"No, why, should I be? What happened?"

"Nothing happened . . . yet. Elina, we're not sending our package in the morning. We're sending me and I need your help."

"What? What do you mean you? You can't go, Alex. We don't know for sure Beatrice is still alive. All we know is that it looked like it worked."

"Truman isn't right there, is he?"

"No. I left the room. Alex, you can't."

"I've made up my mind, Elina. If you won't help me, at least please don't try to stop me. If I don't seize this chance, it will haunt me for the rest of my life."

"You're a good friend, Alex. Of course, I'll help you, if you won't reconsider. In a way, I understand. Don't forget, we intended on telling Dr. Greene and DOD about sending Beatrice. If I tell them about it now, they'll catch on about you, so now what?"

"Well, they'll think I'm nuts for walking away in the first place, so I will let them believe I took her with me. When you think about it, that's not far from the truth; she just beat me there."

I explained about the letter and how I wrote a macro to send it to her and Dr. Greene about a half hour after they believed she first arrived. The macro was then configured to erase itself. I asked Elina to drive to my house when we go. We would take my car to the lab. She would duck down in the back seat and it would look as if only I entered as far as the guard at the gate could see. Once I'm gone, she would drive back to my house and get her car. There's no guard at the exit so they would only see her return later, as if she just got in for the day. I thanked her for agreeing to help me, then set my alarm and tried the best I could to get some sleep. Still tired from the previous night, I fell out for a few hours.

Wednesday June 30th 2010

As I was dressing after my shower, the doorbell rang. I threw a towel around my wet hair and opened the door. Elina was standing there half sad, half angry.

"I can't believe you want to go through with this, Alex."

"You can't change my mind. Please don't even try. Give me a few minutes to dry my hair and we'll go early."

"Well, did you eat?"

"I feel really hungry, but I can't imagine eating right now. Fix something for yourself, if you like."

On the way to SciLab, Elina went from being angry to reminiscing about the past, back to angry. When we were about a mile away, I stopped so that she could get into the back and crouch down. It went well and once we entered the back road, there was no one around. Elina was still careful going into the lab. We talked until it was almost time to start the sequence. I held Elina's arms and looked into her eyes.

"Thank you. You've meant so much to me," I said. "Take good care of yourself, and that great family of yours."

She started to cry and grabbed my face with her palms to kiss my forehead. I walked over to Glint and stepped inside. As the columns closed, I told her to remember, not a word about this to anyone. I told her that if somehow they discover where I'd gone, that she never reveal her involvement. I saw the cloud rise from the columns and felt the magnetic bottle beginning to form. The Alfven waves began and I felt as if I was being stretched from the inside out. I couldn't move and my vision blurred, then I couldn't hear a sound.

Janine arrived early and saw Brice in front of the tavern. She walked over and asked, "Do you have time for a cup of coffee with a friend?"

"Sure I do. Come on in. I'll make a pot."

The lights inside were off except for a lamp at the end of the bar where Brice had his stool. Janine sat on a stool and Brice filled a small coffee pot with water from the sink behind the bar. He noticed the same look on Janine as he earlier saw on Alex.

"Do you want to talk about it?" Brice asked.

"What, about what?"

"Something's troubling you. It's Alex leaving, isn't it?"

"It feels wrong to think about it, but I'm really going to miss him. Cale yelled at me again last night and I thought about what Alex said. He told me that Cale will never change."

"Alex is right."

"So far, none of my relationships have been all that great. I thought it would be different with Cale, but it's not, Brice. For once, why can't I meet a guy as great as Alex?"

"You already did."

The e-mail from Alex reached Dr. Greene's screen and he called Elina into his office. They talked for over an hour as she was asked about what she knew. Elina explained that the tests of Glint were successful and they were ready to demonstrate it to the DOD. She could truthfully say that Alex believed he reached the height of his career and wanted to get away from it all. Greene pointed out in the letter where Alex wrote that Elina would lead and he asked her if she was ready. She assured him she was, and couldn't help becoming teary-eyed. Greene told her they could talk about it more a little later in the day. In the meantime, he would inform the DOD.

On her way out of the main building, Elina passed reception where she recognized Janine at the counter, asking where she might find Alex. Elina intervened and invited her to sit in the waiting area to the side. When she explained that Alex had already gone, Janine cried, and Elina knew she was witnessing what Alex had only dreamed: Janine loved him.

Saturday June 25th 2022 - continued

Elina hoped that in the twelve years of Alex being on WEP, he would have the means to send a message embedded within light. Others would receive and decipher it for sure and it would reveal where he had been all these years, but with Glint successfully deployed, it didn't matter any longer. It went public in twenty-fourteen and some commercial applications were allowed, even if only through license. The DOD started to enlarge Glint for a larger payload. Since Alex left, Elina worked on enhancing Glint through modifications to its subsystems. The original prototype was the only full system in the lab, but she decided to pull it out of mothballs in an attempt to send a message to Alex. She still had the coordinates of his targeted landing site and hoped he would somehow see it. Elina asked Adrian if she could have the feed and went to her lab.

She pulled the tarp off the prototype and started to clean whatever dust seeped underneath. Then, she wheeled out the main panel from back storage, plugging the umbilical into the base of the device. Elina cleaned off the screens. The side screen lit up, but the main screen failed. It would be days before she could patch it together, but if the wormhole remained stable as long as it had in 2010, she could make it work. Elina went to the channel monitor.

"Call Dario, video."

Dario is the maintenance lead at SciLab. She knew how he valued his weekends, but there was little choice. She had to know how long it would take reinstall the large bank of capacitors for Glint They had long been removed and stored in a truck container in back. The channels connected and Dario was rubbing his eyes and had a large mug of coffee on the table in front of him.

"Hi, Elina. Please excuse my scruffiness. The missus and I were out late. What can I do for you?"

"I'm really sorry to bother you on a Saturday, but I need to ask. How long would it take to transport the capacitors back into the lab for Glint?"

"I can do it in a day."

"Please; can you do it Monday? I have a lot of work to do before I need them, but I need to wire them all in. And could we keep this between us?"

"Um, if I wait until Monday, the moving will be noticed, but for you, Elina, I'll be in tomorrow morning."

She called Truman and after not saying a word about it in the last twelve years, she told him what happened to Alex and asked that he understand why she stayed quiet all these years. Truman would have to do without her for now. She explained that she wanted to send Alex a message.

Elina worked late into the night for the next two days, but by Tuesday evening she had all the capacitors wired and started charging the system. She left just after seven to spend time with Truman, thinking of the message she wanted to send to Alex and what items she would include. She felt guilty for keeping Alex's secret for so many years, but Truman understood more than she knew. Because WEP fired a laser in the past, Elina planned to include optical disks of numerous scientific reference materials Alex might find useful, and a video message.

The twenty hours needed to charge Glint for the single shot would take it well beyond the window on Wednesday, so Thursday during the early morning would be the time.

Wednesday June, 29th 2022

Elina still went in at seven AM on Wednesday to pour over the captured feeds, hoping to see some new sign from WEP, and perhaps even a message from Alex. While there was only a narrow access window from where they were located at SciLab, the feed from Sagan was twenty-four hours. Elina knew it was being studied all over the planet, but she still felt compelled to scan the incoming data. First, she stepped up to the wall panel.

"Coffee standard size, dark, one ounce of rice milk."

The panel dispensed her coffee and just as she went to work at her desk, there was a channel connect request from Jordan in the astronomy lab.

"Call connect, video. Good morning, Jordan. Sorry I haven't stopped over, since you got back. Something good?" she asked seeing a grin on his face.

"Look at the feed I'm putting up. I'm going to run it at one-one hundredth speed."

"Multiple laser pulses. In the past, remember, there was only one."

"We're crunching the data to see if there is any significant communications pattern there, but their duration makes it hard to consider an encoded message."

"Jordan, please channel me if you find anything. I think I'll take a look at it myself. Thanks for letting me know."

Elina produced the optical disks and placed them in a small plastic crate normally used to store items on the back shelf. She then walked to her closet and reached up to the top shelf, pulling down Alex's tattered paperback copy of "The Age of Innocence" and placed it on top of the disks. After putting the crate on the pad, she went to her desk and began comparing the data gathered now with what was captured in the past. Several hours into the work she created a graft of the recorded pulses and saw something familiar in the timestamps. Because of that insight, she compared the laser sightings from earlier with the distance and topography study from twelve years ago. When the intervals were plotted and superimposed, they lined up exactly. Because they came from the same source, her colleagues failed to see it thus far.

At that moment, Elina understoodWEP was Earth, and that the wormhole was bridging folded spacetime. It was Earth from the past. It was the fact that lasers were no longer needed for measurement that made her realize that the single shot seen twelve years earlier, days before they sent Beatrice, was her__________. She would fire Glint during the next window, not to send a message, but a location. Elina decided she wouldn't say anything about her discovery. She didn't want anything to disturb the timeline, if that was possible. A warm feeling came over her, because, if she was right, Beatrice would arrive on Friday and Alex the day after.

Elina transferred the remaining data from the past to her flex screen and plotted the time from the test done then, to the time the laser was seen. She accounted for the light minutes and then plotted when Beatrice and Alex should arrive. Hours passed and now early evening, a channel connect request came in from Truman.

"Hi, Elina. I was getting worried about you. Are you coming home?"

"I'm so sorry, Truman. Thanks for taking care of things these past days. I didn't notice the time. I'll be home in the morning, but I have something important to do during the night. I'm just going to get a few hours nap in the lounge."

"I know you are anxious to see some indication from Alex, but I don't want you to get sick."

"It's so much better than an indication. I'll tell you the details in the morning, when I get home."

"Well, can I bring you something to eat?"

"I channeled a place nearby and they will be delivering some salads soon, but thanks. Did I tell you I love you?"

"All the time, but I'll listen any time you want to say it. I love you, too, sweetheart. I'll see you in the morning."

The channel closed and Elina went back to working. But she also channeled for the salads she told Truman she already ordered. Soon there were containers and flex screens all over her desk and she went to the lounge to nap for a few hours, careful to set an indicator and another on her portable to be sure.

Thursday June, 30th 2022

It felt to her as if she just closed her eyes, when the indicator sounded. Once awake enough, Elina remembered what was happening, and savored the thought. She checked all the systems and shut down the magnetic containment and wave pulse. She would only send light. It fired perfectly and there was nothing to do until tomorrow so she went home and slept until three-forty-five in the afternoon. Truman was stunned, when she told him what she'd discovered and done. He asked if she would like him to go with her, but Elina thought it best she be there alone. After Truman cooked her a large meal of salmon, asparagus and salad, she went back to sleep.

Friday July 1st 2022

Elina woke at two-forty-five, close to the time Beatrice would be sent; although it would be one hundred and forty minutes until she arrived. She showered and dressed, stuffed a bag full of fruit from the kitchen and left. She arrived and retracted the roof, hearing a slight strain on the large chains around the motor. Dario kept the motor maintained, but with little use all these years it needed to be replaced. She cleared over two meters all around Glint and then waited and watched. Just before five AM, Elina saw a light hit the floor to the side, just off the pad. Beatrice materialized bottom-up, taking just a few moments. She was disoriented and was focusing on nothing. It was obvious her vision was blurred as it was after her transport to Shawangunk years ago. Elina sat on the floor and spoke to Beatrice, touching her arm. Beatrice wrapped her arms around Elina's waist and placed her head sideways deep in Elina's chest. Only a few minutes passed before it was clear that Beatrice could see again. She was the same ten year old Orangutan that Elina remembered.

Beatrice was happy with Elina playing with her for hours longer than she had done in the past. To Beatrice, that past was only minutes before she arrived. She did look around a few times, apparently hoping to see Alex, but she would see him soon enough. The outside pen Beatrice enjoyed was long ago dismantled, but the inside room was still fairly empty with just a few storage bins stacked up against the wall. Elina gave her the fruit and locked her inside. After closing the roof and wall panels, Elina left. This time she couldn't sleep until evening.

Saturday July 2nd 2022

Just after two AM, Elina showered and dressed then snuck downstairs quietly, so as not to wake Truman and the girls. She again stuffed fruit into a bag and went to the panel to request coffee to take with her for the drive to SciLab. On the drive she thought of all the changes in the last twelve years that were sure to shock Alex. She entered the SciLab gate and as she drove up the road, the lights went on and then off behind her car. Elina's car was almost silent and with an open window she could hear the sounds of night in the valley just behind the lab. Once inside she retracted the roof and wall and then went in to see Beatrice.

With still an hour to go, Elina pulled a chair just outside of the area around the pad and sat to wait. Her smile grew stronger as the time grew nearer. Then the room lit up with the laser and Alex began to materialize near the edge of the pad.

I feel numb, I accept that I'm awake, but my vision is distorted and I can't hear. Where am I? What am I doing on the floor? What is that shape moving my way? My name is Alex. I know my name is Alex. It's getting closer. I feel it wrapping around me. The numbness is beginning to fade and I can feel someone's arms. My vision is still unclear, but I hear something.

"Alex."

I heard my name and the voice seemed familiar, then I heard it several more times. I'm beginning to remember who I am. It's Elina's voice, and her arms are holding me. I'm trying desperately to speak.

"Elina," I said softly.

"Alex. You're OK. You'll feel normal again in a few minutes. Your sight will return shortly as well."

"What happened to me?"

"You rode Glint."

Hearing the name, I started to remember.

"I do remember now, but what happened? Why didn't it work?"

"But it did work, Alex. It worked perfectly."

My eyes began to focus and I saw a room full of things unfamiliar to me. I sat up and turned toward Elina. It was her, but…

Seeing a directed look in my eyes, Elina said, "You're home, Alex. I missed you. Glint worked perfectly. We were unaware that WEP was Earth. The wormhole was a bridge though folded spacetime. We sent you twelve years ago. Welcome to twenty twenty-two."

I smiled and started to look around the room and picking up objects from the table. There were very few buttons on anything.

"Wait, Beatrice. What happened to Beatrice?"

"She's fine. Beatrice arrived yesterday. She's in her room; well, what was her room. I gave her plenty of food and water. We'll look in on her in a minute."

"This is too amazing. It looks like technology really advanced. And you look great, Elina. Life has been good to you."

"Thanks. I appreciate that. When you left you were thinking your life was over. We're the same age now, Alex, so no more of that, OK?" Elina said with a mild laugh.

I asked about the large flat panels and some of the other small items on the table. Elina turned on the panels and they were incredibly high resolution video screens. What most caught my attention was when she explained about a small handheld device she called her portable. It did everything and the concept of having a channel was fascinating. It was a personal link to video, audio, data, whatever. It made the web/phone devices of the past look like antiques. I asked about Truman and the girls and Elina went into overdrive, telling me about all the girl's achievements over the years. But it wasn't much later when she noticed I looked emotionally drained.

"Let's get you out of here," Elina said. You can see Beatrice when we come back. I'm taking you home."

"Home?"

"Since you wrote the letter, no one had cause to touch your property. I remembered when you were happy your town withdrew taxes so they never touched it either."

"There wasn't time or I would have turned my assets over to you."

"Truman, the girls and I live in Tuxedo Park. Glint is being used by a select group of corporations under license, but with severe restrictions. DOD gets a share for its investment; SciLab gets a portion as do I, while the lions share has been accumulating in your account."

"I would bet I owe quite a bit in back taxes," I said and laughed.

"Not on your share from Glint. I arranged to have taxes removed before funds are deposited in your account, although you're quite in the rears with your returns," she said smiling.

We left and I was amazed at the technology in Elina's car. It was powered by fuel cell and the materials inside made it all but silent. The back road had a few more buildings on it and there were many more homes on Clove Road as we drove toward Salisbury Mills. So many of the cars look as strange as Elina's, but now and then an older one passed that looked familiar. She turned up my driveway and when we reached the house, I could see it was sorely in need of maintenance. Elina lifted the garage door and reached into my car to retrieve my keys thrown there on the day she dropped it off. I walked to the side and pressed the button for the generator.

It struggled, but it finally started and we opened the front door to go in. The door stuck for a moment, shoving the large pile of junk mail that had been pushed through the mail slot. Elina told me unsolicited mail was banned almost five years ago or the pile would have been even larger.

To me, I'd left just hours ago, but there was dust everywhere. Elina helped me clean the kitchen, bathroom and living room, while we talked about many of the changes that occurred. Cleaning inside the cabinets, she laughed when she saw my CD player, just as she did when she saw my laptop on the desk in the living room. I turned on the player and pressed eject to see the Michaelson CD still in the drive, but covered in dust. I was scrubbing the inside of the refrigerator, when Elina thought to order food for me and barely two hours passed before the delivery was brought to my door. It was enough to fill the refrigerator and one cabinet. By early evening there were two rooms clean enough to live in.

"I have to go now, Alex. We should talk with Dr. Greene, when you feel up to it. Take a couple days to get acclimated; he'll be in his office on Tuesday, after the holiday. Here, I want you to take this. I have another at home."

She handed me her portable and told me she set up a channel for me. The charge would last for days, but she explained I would need a charging pad. Elina helped me link the device to my accounts and I was stunned at the amount of money in them. She showed me how to connect to the utility companies and when I placed a request to turn on the electric service, the verification message stated that power would be restored within the hour. Lastly, she demonstrated how things are purchased. Touching the upper right side of the frame, followed by holding the portable up to a grey bar with a blue LED completes the transaction.

"Thanks, Elina. Thanks for being there for me all this time and for helping me settle in. Remember, not a word about your involvement. I did this on my own."

She hugged me and told me she would check on me tomorrow. She said she would take me to buy a new car on Monday. There would be holiday sales, but money was something I would never have to worry about. I walked her out and watched until she was out of sight. I washed and dried a load of clothes, then heated a meal of eggplant and poured some orange juice to take into the living room. I fell asleep scanning through the public channels, trying to learn about current events.

Sunday July 3rd 2022

I woke just before seven AM and dug through the closet next to the bathroom to find my old electric razor. The handled razor heads had long rusted. After a shower I dressed, clipped the portable on my belt and decided to go for a walk before breakfast. I made a right on Route 94 and was soon halfway into town, so I decided to go all the way. I was curious to see how much had changed and I hoped that Brooks Tavern would still be there. I was excited that I might see Brice. When I reached the edge of town, the street was lined with flags and banners, and the gazebo and clock tower on the Moffett Library were welcome sights. Most all of the stores had changed, but until I turned onto the triangle I wouldn't know if I'd see Brooks. What had been the computer repair shop now sported a 3-D sign that read, tech repair. There was a shop for portables where the auto parts store was, and there was a deli, but everything in the window displays looked unfamiliar. When I reached the town triangle, I saw over a dozen people decorating for the holiday. Brooks was still there and Brice was trying to unfold a table in front. While he was still pulling out a folded leg, I took hold of the other side.

"Here, I'll help you with that," I said.

Brice looked up, "Alex! Alex! I thought we'd never see you again. You look exactly the same as I remember."

"Healthy living," I said and laughed. "It's a long story. It looks like the years have been kind to you as well, my friend"

We finished up-righting the table and he put his arm around me, walking me inside. The place looked exactly the same. It was as clean as it had always been and we took our spots at the end of the bar.

"Can I make you some coffee, Alex?"

"That would be great. I see the town is going all out for Independence Day."

"You know I've always been set in my ways, but it seems as if the more complicated life gets, the more people need celebrations."

"How is your daughter doing?"

"She lost her husband in an accident last year, but she's doing better now. Harry had two daughters who were no different to Lacie than if they were her own. They've always been like granddaughters to me. The older girl, Kaela, eventually helped Lacie through it. You know; Kaela works in that place where you used to work."

The front door opened and a girl of eleven or twelve walked in and over to Brice.

"We need more balloons, Mr. Brooks. Do you have any left?"

He crouched down to open the cabinet and, while the young girl was eyeing me up and down, he handed her a bag filled with red, white and blue balloons.

"Alexandra, this is Alex. Alex; Alexandra," Brice said.

"It's nice to meet you, Alexandra," I said.

"Call me Alex," she told me. I don't see a ring. You're not married, huh?"

Brice responded, "Alexandra, please stop trying to marry off your mother. Alex; you may remember her mother."

The front door opened and still turned away, I heard a woman call, "Alex."

Alexandra and I both turned. It was Janine coming in. She was more beautiful than ever and when she saw me, it took a moment for her to catch her breath.

"Alex. I can't believe it's you. I'd given up hope I would ever see you again. You look great. You look the same as you did when you left. Exactly the same."

"I'll have to explain it to you, but you may find it hard to believe."

Alexandra interrupted, "You look great too, Mom. Doesn't she look great for forty, Alex?"

“More beautiful than I could have imagined.”

Looking pleased with herself, Alexandra said “bye” and as she passed Brice I glanced over to see her look at him with a deep smile.

Janine and I walked over to sit in the first booth to talk, but for a few moments we only stared at each other.

“Alexandra’s a handful, but she’s a great kid,” Janine said obviously proud. “Her father is Cale. He moved to Florida just after she was born and I’ve raised her on my own ever since. You were right about him. Some people never change. …Have you changed, Alex?”

“My feelings are exactly the same as the last time I saw you.”

Breinigsville, PA USA
19 March 2010

234494BV00003B/1/P